SCOOBY-DOO! AND THE SCARY SKATEBOARDER

Written by
James Gelsey

A
LITTLE APPLE
PAPERBACK

SCHOLASTIC INC.

New York   Toronto   London   Auckland   Sydney
Mexico City   New Delhi   Hong Kong   Buenos Aires

ISBN 0-439-56117-5

Designed by Michael Massen

12 11 10 9 8 7 6 5 4 3 2   6 7 8 9 10/0

Special thanks to Duendes del Sur for cover and interior
illustrations.

Printed in the U.S.A.
First printing, March 2006

Chapter 1

Scooby-Doo, Shaggy, and the rest of the gang were enjoying a restful afternoon in Pollywog Park. They had just finished solving a big case and decided to take the day off to relax. Pollywog Park was an enormous park famous for its vast green fields and shimmering blue lake.

Shaggy and Scooby lazed in a rowboat in the middle of the Great Pollywog Pond. As they drifted along, the big clock atop the boat-house chimed three times. The two friends immediately perked up.

"Three o'clock, Scoob," Shaggy said. "You know what that means?"

Scooby knew. He remembered that Fred, Daphne, and Velma had told them they'd all meet up for ice cream at three o'clock.

"Rice cream!" Scooby barked. "Rippee!"

Shaggy lifted an oar and began paddling the little rowboat across the lake. "Uh, Scoob, if you don't grab an oar, man, we'll be going in circles all day," he said. Scooby took an oar and began rowing with his friend.

"Man, I know just what I'm going to get," Shaggy said dreamily. "Like, I'm gonna have the biggest tutti-frutti rocky-roady cookie-doughy ice-cream sundae you've ever seen!"

Scooby's big pink tongue licked his lips as he pictured Shaggy's amazing ice-cream treat.

"Reah, ree roo." He nodded eagerly. "Raster, Raggy!"

Scooby dropped the oar and began rowing with his big Scooby paws. He and Shaggy got into a rhythm that moved the rowboat along faster and faster. They were so caught up in rowing and dreaming about ice cream that they didn't hear the shouts of the two men in the boat in front of them.

"Hey! Slow down!" one of them called.

"Watch out!" the other yelled.

Shaggy and Scooby turned their heads.

"Zoinks!" Shaggy cried. "Like, put on the brakes, Scoob!"

But rowboats don't have brakes. So Shaggy and Scooby did the next best thing: They covered their eyes and screamed. They expected to ram right into the other rowboat, but then one . . . two . . . three seconds passed without incident. They each opened one eye for a peek.

"Like, what happened?" Shaggy wondered. "Where's the boat?"

As their rowboat floated up to the dock, Shaggy and Scooby scanned the lake. There was no sign of the other rowboat, so Shaggy checked the big clock on top of the boathouse.

"Three-oh-two," he reported. "Man, I hope they don't run out of ice cream!"

As the two friends made their way down the dock, Shaggy noticed two men climbing out of a rowboat. One was tall and dressed in a green suit. The other wore a brown suit and was somewhat stouter.

"Look, Scoob, it's the guys from that rowboat we almost hit!" Shaggy said. He walked up to them and apologized. "Like, sorry about what happened back there. It's just that me and my pal here were so excited about our three o'clock ice-cream date that we sort of got carried away."

Scooby gave each of the men a quick lick on the cheek.

"That's all right," said the tall man. Scooby noticed the man had a little goatee just like Shaggy. "We have to be somewhere at three o'clock also."

"Good thing we were able to toss our towrope to the dockhands," the other man said. His brown suit sported a blue and yellow handkerchief in the chest pocket. "They pulled our boat out of the way just in time."

"Speaking of time," the taller man said, "I think it's time we were off. We're already . . ."

He raised his left arm to check his watch. But when he looked down at his wrist, he gasped. "Oh, dear! My watch must have fallen off in the rowboat!"

He and the short man in the brown suit ran back down the dock.

"I wonder if their three o'clock meeting was going to be as sweet and tasty as ours," Shaggy said.

"Ri runno," Scooby shrugged.

"You're right, pal o' mine," Shaggy said. "Who cares about anything else when ice cream is on the way? Last one to the end of the dock is a soggy ice-cream cone!"

Chapter 2

Shaggy and Scooby ran to the end of the dock and came to an abrupt stop. The cement path led off into the park in three different directions. Shaggy and Scooby didn't know which one to take to the ice-cream stand.

"Man, I can't believe this," Shaggy moaned. "It's already three-oh-five! We're late for, like, the most important part of our day!"

"Not anymore!" said a voice from behind them.

Shaggy and Scooby turned and saw a young woman standing there. Strands of brown hair dangled out from beneath her purple and

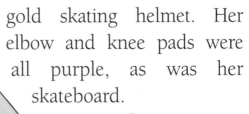

gold skating helmet. Her elbow and knee pads were all purple, as was her skateboard.

"I'm Sabrina Sargent. I came over to make sure you didn't get lost," she said. "Seems like I arrived just in time, too. After all, we can't start without you."

Shaggy and Scooby were relieved to hear that they hadn't missed any ice cream.

"Like, it's really cool of you to come get us and everything," Shaggy said. "But who are you? A friend of Fred's or something?"

Sabrina looked a little puzzled at the question but smiled, anyway. "I don't know who Fred is, but everyone's over at the skate park," Sabrina said, leading the way.

"That's a funny place for an ice-cream stand," Shaggy said to Scooby.

"Oh, there's a full snack bar complex there," Sabrina said. "We've got a juice bar, a salad station, and even a coffeehouse. There'll be plenty of time for ice cream after you're done."

Shaggy and Scooby looked at each other.

"Like, after we're done with what?" asked Shaggy.

"Judging the big skateboard contest, of course!" Sabrina said.

Shaggy and Scooby followed Sabrina through Pollywog Park. Sabrina zipped along on her skateboard in front of Shaggy and Scooby.

"Like, did you say 'judge a skateboard contest'?" Shaggy asked.

Sabrina nodded. "I forgot you had mentioned in your e-mail that you were going boating before the contest," she said. "I must admit, I was a little worried about finding you. It's a

9

good thing you sent us that e-mail with what you were wearing. Otherwise I might have taken the wrong people!" Sabrina laughed as she took a slip of paper from her pocket and held it out for Shaggy.

"I'll be wearing a green top and my friend will be in brown," Shaggy read aloud from the page. He looked down at his long green shirt and at Scooby's brown fur.

"Man, I think this lady's got her wires crossed," Shaggy whispered to his friend.

"Here we are!" Sabrina announced as she skidded to a stop beneath a metal archway.

Shaggy and Scooby looked up and saw the enormous silver sign spanning the entrance to the skate park.

"'Pollywog Skaters' Paradise,'" Shaggy said, reading the shiny sign on the arch. A pair of skateboarders zipped past them.

"You two wait over there," Sabrina said. "I'll go make sure everything's ready."

Sabrina skated off to a small pavilion with a big banner plastered on its side. The poster featured a giant skateboard coming right at them, with the outline of a skate park in the background.

"We have to find Fred, Daphne, and Velma," Shaggy said to Scooby. "Like, now! Let's make a run for it while we can." Shaggy and Scooby turned and headed for the archway. As they did, however, music started blasting from loud-speakers. The music was like a call to the skaters, and hundreds of them began pouring into the skate park. Shaggy and Scooby were unable to fight against the rolling tide. A particularly large skateboarder bumped right into them and went on his way without so much as an apology.

"That wasn't very nice!" came a familiar voice from the crowd.

"Daphne!" Shaggy cried. "Are we glad to see you!"

Fred, Daphne, and Velma walked over to Shaggy and Scooby.

"Where were you two?" Velma asked. "Don't tell me that the unthinkable happened — that you two actually forgot about a chance to eat."

Shaggy and Scooby quickly shook their heads.

"Ruh-uh," Scooby barked.

"Man, me and Scoob were on our way for ice cream when this girl on wheels came by and took us here," Shaggy explained. "I think she thinks we're here to do something that has nothing to do with delicious dairy desserts."

Before any of the others could comment, Sabrina Sargent returned.

"We're just about all set," she said. "The skaters are gathering in the back to go over the rules and stuff. You two will be sitting on the judging platform over there."

She pointed to a wooden platform that was perched on top of the pavilion with the banner. A table and two chairs stood on the platform beneath a wide blue and yellow umbrella.

"Excuse me, but did you say 'judging platform'?" Velma asked.

Sabrina nodded.

"Well, you two," Fred said with a smile, "you've certainly done it this time!"

Chapter 3

"Like, we had nothing to do with it!" Shaggy protested.

"I'm sorry, but what's going on here?" Sabrina asked.

Daphne explained that she thought Sabrina must have made some kind of mistake because Shaggy and Scooby were not qualified to be skateboard judges.

"But they fit the description that the two guys from the skateboard company gave us," Sabrina said. She held out the e-mail. "See? Green and brown."

Shaggy suddenly remembered the other two guys on the dock — the ones whose boat they almost hit. He cleared his throat and told the others what had happened.

Realizing her mistake, Sabrina turned to go. "I have to find the real judges before we begin!" she said.

"Not so fast, Sabrina Sargent!" boomed a voice. It was the large man who had bumped into Shaggy and Scooby earlier. "I've got a bone to pick with you!"

The large man on the skateboard rolled over to Sabrina. Even without his skateboard, he would have towered over her. But standing on his board made him look even loftier. He stared down at Sabrina, his muscles bulging beneath his tight-fitting racing jersey.

"W-w-what can I do for you, Wheels?" Sabrina asked.

"What can you do for me?" he echoed. "You can start by explaining why I, Wheels Trackman, have to skate with all those runny-nosed little skateboard runts. And then you can tell me when I, Wheels Trackman, will have my solo! After all, I, Wheels Trackman, do not take kindly to sharing."

Sabrina regained her composure. "I am so sorry, Wheels. You are absolutely right," she said. "I know everyone here is exceedingly grateful that a skateboard star of your caliber agreed to come celebrate the opening of the skate park. Once things get started, I'm sure we'll be able to sort everything out."

Wheels Trackman studied Sabrina's face as he weighed her words. The anger seemed to drain out of his eyes, at least for the moment.

"Fine, but I, Wheels Trackman, am still not happy, and won't be until things are settled," he warned. "And no one wants Wheels Trackman to be unhappy."

He put one foot on his board as if to warn the group that he was about to skate away. And sure enough, with one push of his other leg, he took off on his skateboard. As he rode away, he somersaulted into the air and landed back on his board.

"He may be a royal pain, but he's good," Sabrina said.

"So are you," Daphne said. "You handled him pretty well. I never knew that skaters could be so vain."

"Most of them are great folks," Sabrina said. "That's why I wanted to work here at the skate park. The people are just so friendly. But every once in a while you get a bad wheel."

"Like Wheels Trackman?" asked Fred.

"Wheels? He's not a bad wheel — he's like a whole skate park full of trouble," Sabrina joked. The others laughed until a pale, angry man in a black T-shirt and pants walked up to Sabrina.

"You want trouble? I'll give you trouble, all right," he said to her.

Sabrina rolled her eyes and sighed.

"Don't you roll your eyes at me, missy," he scolded. "I've got some papers here that may interest you."

He waved a fistful of crumpled white pages in the air. But before he could continue, Fred stepped forward and stood between him and

Sabrina. "No reason to wave a fistful of crumpled papers around," he said.

The man looked Fred up and down. "Who are you?" asked the man.

Fred introduced himself and the rest of the gang. Then he asked the man the same question.

"Gregory Bly," the man said. "I own Arcadeland down the street."

Sabrina then explained that Gregory Bly wanted to use the skate park to help drum up business for his video arcade.

"See, I even had a thousand special video tokens minted for the occasion," he said, showing the gang a golden coin. The word *Arcadeland* appeared on one side and a picture of Wheels Trackman on the other.

"He developed some kind of video game with Wheels in it," Sabrina said.

"Wheels loved it!" Gregory announced. "He also loved the token I gave him yesterday."

"Wheels loved the free publicity," Sabrina replied. "But since the skate park won't help Mr. Bly advertise his arcade, he's angry at us."

"Darn tootin'!" Gregory replied. "It cost a lot of money to make these tokens. And I haven't been able to use a single one of them, thanks to you. Everyone's coming here instead of Arcadeland. And not only that, I spent a fortune on computer gaming chips that I can plug into any video game to make it a Wheels Trackman video game. I took all of my skating experience from when I was a kid and put it into that game."

Sabrina shook her head. "The skate park is all about getting people outside in the fresh air to exercise and have fun," she said. "We don't want people standing in dark rooms playing with overgrown television sets."

Gregory Bly was clearly offended by Sabrina's comments. He puffed out his chest angrily and waved the fistful of papers again.

"We'll see about all that," he warned. "These are copies of the town's zoning bylaws. I have it on good authority that this skate park is violating several safety regulations. If I find anything like that, I'll close you down for good!"

As Gregory Bly stormed away, the gang watched him stuff the papers in his right pocket and take a small video game from his left pocket. Almost instantly, he became completely engrossed in the game.

"Now there's someone who could use some fresh air and exercise," Daphne said.

A young boy on a skateboard rode over to Sabrina.

"They're ready to begin," he told her.

"Thanks," Sabrina said. She looked at Shaggy and Scooby.

"Sorry to do this to you, but how about it?" she asked. "Ready to judge your very first skateboard competition?"

"Like, why not?" Shaggy shrugged. "What could possibly go wrong?"

Chapter 4

As Shaggy and Scooby followed Sabrina, a rather frumpy-looking older woman walked toward Fred, Daphne, and Velma. She wore a flowered housecoat and high-top sneakers. Her attention was focused on some papers she was holding. As a result, she plowed right into Fred, sending her papers — and Fred — flying.

"Oh, my!" the woman exclaimed. "I am so sorry! Please forgive me!" She reached down and helped Fred stand back up. "Are you all right, sonny?"

Fred nodded. "Yes, I'm fine," he replied.

"Oh, dear me," the woman continued. "I

am such a klutz. I have not been myself lately. I've done nothing but worry, worry, worry, morning, noon, and night." She realized that Fred, Daphne, and Velma all had worried looks on their faces. The woman smiled.

"Listen to me, going on and on," she sighed. "I must sound like a crazy lady to you kids. I'm Harriet Higgenbotham."

She extended her hand in greeting. Daphne, Velma, and Fred each shook her hand and introduced themselves.

"So, if you don't mind our asking, what are you so worried about?" asked Daphne.

Harriet Higgenbotham nodded sadly. "This place," she said. "I live in the red house on the other side of the wall over there." She pointed in the direction of the far side of the skate park. "When they were building this place, they wanted me to move so they could make the park even bigger. But I refused because I grew up in that house. Pollywog Park has been my

backyard for over sixty years, and I didn't see any reason to have to move."

"Jinkies!" Velma gasped. "You've lived in the same house for sixty years? That's very impressive."

"It's been heavenly," Harriet said. "But not anymore. There's so much noise from those irksome skateboarders that I can't get a moment's peace. I can't count how many times I've asked them to keep it down. Now I've had to resort to studying the town's zoning bylaws to see if those skaters are violating local noise ordinances. I'm at my wit's end."

Fred, Daphne, and Velma shook their heads in pity for Harriet Higgenbotham.

"Sounds pretty bad," Fred agreed. A quick glance at Daphne and Velma told Fred that it was time to go. "Well, it was nice meeting you, but we —"

Harriet Higgenbotham interrupted Fred with even more of her sob story. "And it's not just me, you know," she continued. "That nice Mr. Bly at the arcade down the street — his business is suffering, too, because of this skate park. Why, I was in there just yesterday and he showed me this lovely new video game with some skating hotshot. I think his name was Tires or Axles or something like that."

"You mean Wheels Trackman?" Velma asked.

Harriet nodded enthusiastically. "Yes, that's

it!" she said. "And that nice Mr. Bly even gave me one of those special tokens. Yes, that arcade's the only place I can go around here for some peace and quiet."

Those words struck Fred, Daphne, and Velma as somewhat unusual.

"But isn't the arcade even louder than the skate park?" Daphne asked.

Harriet Higgenbotham seemed not to hear Daphne.

"Well, I've kept you young people quite long enough," she said. "You're very kind to indulge an old woman like me. You three

have a good afternoon now." As she trotted off, Fred, Daphne, and Velma looked at one another. They searched for words to describe their encounter with Harriet Higgenbotham.

"Unusual," Fred said.

"Puzzling," Velma said.

"Freaky," Daphne said.

The three nodded in laughter.

"Speaking of freaky, we should see how Shaggy and Scooby are doing," Velma suggested.

A fanfare blasted through the loudspeakers all over the skate park.

"Sounds like the opening ceremony is about to begin," Fred said. "Let's go."

Chapter 5

Fred, Daphne, and Velma spied an open spot along a metal railing and walked through the crowd and over to it. The railing ran around the entire top of the skate park, which was sunken into the ground below.

"Nice set of pipes," Fred said admiringly.

"Pardon me?" Velma said.

"Pipes," Fred repeated. "That's what they call the skating area. That's because most of them are shaped like giant pipes, see?" He pointed to the various skating surfaces. Velma realized that all of the curved surfaces were in fact like sections of gigantic concrete pipes. "That's a

half-pipe," Fred said, pointing to a long U-shaped piece of concrete. "And that's a quarter-pipe."

Velma and Daphne noticed the crescent-shaped pipe. Daphne also noticed two staircases that rose up from opposite ends of the pit.

"Those steps help the skaters get back up here," she said.

At the opposite side of the pit, they noticed the pavilion with the wooden judging platform on top. There, sitting beneath a blue and yellow umbrella, were Shaggy and Scooby-Doo. Sabrina Sargent stood beside them.

"I can't believe they're really doing this," Daphne said.

"Should be very interesting," Velma added.

The crowd quieted down as Sabrina began to speak.

"Welcome, everyone!" she shouted.

The crowd erupted in cheers and whistles. At that moment, six skaters launched themselves down into the pipes. Two of the skaters veered off to the left, and two to the right. The ones in the middle soared straight down and up the far side of the pipe where they each went into a McTwist. The two on the left and right each performed perfect 540's before coming back down onto the ramp. The crowd roared their approval.

As the skaters began a complicated routine of crisscrossing one another along the quarter-pipe, an ear-piercing scraping sound filled the pit. One by one, the skateboards ground to a halt and the riders stumbled to the ground.

"Look! Their wheels are coming off!" a spectator shouted.

Fred, Daphne, and Velma looked closely at the skaters in the pit and saw that the spectator was right.

"Those skateboarders are losing their wheels!" Daphne gasped.

The skateboarders down below looked at their skateboards in disbelief. As they gathered up their wheels, a rumbling filled the skate pit. The sound grew louder until a thunderous roar erupted throughout the park. A masked skateboarder burst through the crowd and sailed over the metal railing. The skateboarder was draped in a black cape and wore a golden mask that glistened in the sunlight. Its black and gold skateboard threw off sparks. As it skated around the pit, it bellowed out a warning.

"Skaters, your days here are numbered!" it announced ominously. "Four wheels become three, and skating can't be. Three judges become two, and what will you do? Two

32

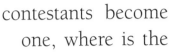

contestants become one, where is the fun? And when one park closes down, all is right in the town."

And with that mysterious rhyme echoing through the air, the Skate Monster soared back up the ramp and over the metal guardrail. The crowd was abuzz — the frightening monster was actually an amazing skater! Suddenly the monster made its way to the judging platform and snatched Sabrina Sargent away!

"Zoinks! Skate Monster!" Shaggy cried. "He wins!" Shaggy held up a scorecard with the number 10 on it. "Let's go, Scooby. Our job here is done!"

Shaggy and Scooby jumped off the platform and slid down the half-pipe. They continued up the other side and came to a stop right in front of where Fred, Daphne, and Velma were standing.

"Well, fellas, it looks like you've found yourselves right in the middle of a mystery!" Velma said.

Chapter 6

When the Skate Monster disappeared with Sabrina, the crowd realized that it meant business. The skaters rolled out as fast as they could, and within minutes the place was completely deserted. The gang gathered behind the main pavilion to get themselves organized.

"If we're going to figure out who's behind Sabrina's kidnapping, we'd better split up to look for clues," Fred said.

Daphne and Velma nodded in agreement.

"And the sooner, the better," Daphne added.

"I say we check out the half-pipe first," Velma suggested. She figured that the monster would most likely have dropped something while executing all of those complicated skating moves.

"Sounds good, Velma," Fred agreed. "Why don't you take Shaggy and Scooby down with you? Daphne and I will look around up here and by the judges' platform."

Shaggy and Scooby followed Velma to one of the long staircases that led down to the bottom of the skate pit. As they descended, Shaggy leaned over toward Scooby.

"Man, I don't know about you, Scooby-Doo, but what I wouldn't give to be rowing around that lake again," he whispered.

Scooby nodded. "Reah, ree roo," he replied.

Velma looked over her shoulder at the friends. "Come on, fellas, it's not so bad here," she said. Velma walked out into the middle of the skate pit. The sides of the half-pipe curved up around her. Visibly impressed, Velma nodded in appreciation of the half-pipe's design.

"It's deceptively simple," she said. "The curvature of the pipe provides skaters with the momentum they need to execute tricks that appear to defy gravity. But spending more time in the air means they need to spend more time riding the pipe to generate the energy. This is very interesting."

Shaggy and Scooby lost interest in Velma's explanation after the word *simple*. Instead they focused their attention on the skate wheels that were littering the ground down there.

Shaggy picked up a wheel and rolled it as hard as he could. It rolled about two feet up the side of the pipe before turning sideways and sliding back down. He and Scooby looked at each other and smiled. Without saying a word, they each grabbed as many wheels as they could and began rolling them up the pipe.

"C'mon, Scoob, faster!" Shaggy urged. Scooby sprang into action, even using his tail to help.

Velma saw what Shaggy and Scooby were doing. She rolled her eyes and shook her head. "Would you two cut it out?" she asked. "We're supposed to be looking for clues. Besides, those wheels could provide valuable information. Why don't you two gather them up so I can examine them?"

Shaggy and Scooby grabbed the wheels as they slid back down the pipe and brought them over to Velma. She gave the wheels a quick

once-over and nodded as if to confirm something she already knew.

"All of these wheels are perfectly intact," she said. "That means our Skate Monster was probably in the skate park before the competition began. It had plenty of time to loosen these wheels just enough so they would fall off soon after the skaters started going."

"But, like, couldn't that have been any-body?" Shaggy asked.

Velma agreed that her conclusion didn't really get them any closer to finding suspects. "But it's a good first step," she said. "Let's go see if Fred and Daphne found anything."

Shaggy and Scooby were extremely happy to hear they were leaving the skate pit, so they raced over to the stairs. They both reached the steps at the same time and got stuck trying to squeeze through the handrails.

"Tell you what, Scoob," Shaggy said. "I'll flip you for it. Heads, I'm first. Tails, you're last."

"Rokay!" Scooby barked.

Shaggy took a coin from his pocket and flipped it into the air. He fumbled the catch, and the coin rolled over to where Velma was standing. She bent down and looked at the coin.

"Where did you get this coin, Shaggy?" she asked.

"Like, right over there," he said, pointing to the place where he and Scooby had been rolling the wheels.

Velma picked up the coin and examined it closely. "This is no ordinary coin, Shaggy," she said.

"How do you know?" Shaggy asked.

"The coins I'm familiar with all have presidents on them," she said. "And I don't think Wheels Trackman was ever elected president." She held up the coin and showed Shaggy and Scooby that it was really a token from Arcadeland.

"Good job, fellas," Velma said. "You just found our first clue."

Chapter 7

Velma, Shaggy, and Scooby spied Fred and Daphne on the judging platform. Daphne motioned for them to come up.

"It looks like Fred and Daphne have something to show us," Velma said.

When Velma, Shaggy, and Scooby climbed up to the judges' platform, Velma got right down to business. "What did you find?" she asked Daphne and Fred.

"You mean besides a bunch of empty potato chip bags?" Daphne said, giving Shaggy and Scooby a look.

"Like, Sabrina said she didn't want the

judges getting hungry during the competition, so they gave us snacks," Shaggy explained.

"Reah, rummy snacks," Scooby said, licking his lips.

"Well, we did find this," Fred said. "It looks like our Skate Monster is a poet in training."

He handed Velma a wrinkled piece of paper. It was covered with words and cross-outs.

Velma brought it closer to her eyes and read what she could.

"'Four wheels, meals, deals. Four wheels

become three, no skating . . .'" Velma said. "This looks like the paper the Skate Monster used to practice writing its creepy rhyme."

"And that's not all," Fred said. "Check out the other side."

Velma flipped the page over and saw words at the top of the printed page. "'Zoning by-laws,'" she read. "Wow! Another great clue."

Velma showed Fred and Daphne the token that Shaggy and Scooby had found earlier.

"These two clues are really helpful," Daphne said.

"But we still need more information to be certain about who's behind all this," Velma said. "We've got to keep looking."

Shaggy's face suddenly lit up. "I've got a great idea!" he said. "Why don't Scooby and I look for clues at the ice-cream stand?"

Fred, Daphne, and Velma stared at Shaggy blankly.

"And how would that help us solve this mystery and find Sabrina?" asked Daphne.

"It won't, but it's still a great idea," Shaggy said. "Right, Scoob?"

Scooby excitedly shook his head in agreement. "Ret's ro!" he barked.

"Nice try, fellas," Velma said. "But we need your help here."

"And if you don't want to help look for clues, at least you can try to track down Sabrina," Fred said.

Shaggy and Scooby knew that Fred was right, so they climbed down from the judges' platform and began their search.

"Like, if you were a skateboard monster, Scooby, where would you hide someone you kidnapped?" Shaggy asked his furry friend.

Scooby rested his chin on his right forepaw and scratched his head with his left forepaw. "Hmmmmmm," Scooby wondered, thinking about Shaggy's question.

Shaggy leaned up against the side of the pavilion while he thought about it as well.

Suddenly, Shaggy felt something shift along the wall. He jumped into Scooby's arms.

"It's alive!" Shaggy shrieked. "The wall's alive!"

"Ruh-roh!" Scooby gasped, trying to run away. But Shaggy was too heavy, so all Scooby could do was run in place. After about a minute of that, they both realized that the wall wasn't really alive.

"Man, it's a hidden doorway!" Shaggy said. "What better place for a monster to hide someone? I'll bet Sabrina Sargent's right inside. Come out, Sabrina, the coast is clear!"

Shaggy folded his arms in triumph and turned to face Scooby.

"You know, pal, Fred, Daphne, and Velma think they've got all the crime-solving smarts," Shaggy said. "But they always overlook little you-know-who."

Scooby looked over Shaggy's shoulder and his eyes nearly bugged out of his head. "Raggy?" Scooby said.

"What is it, my canine companion?" Shaggy asked.

"Rit's not Rabrina," Scooby said.

"What do you mean 'it's not Sabrina'?" Shaggy asked. "Who else could it be tucked away behind a hidden door?"

"Rate Ronster!" Scooby barked.

Chapter 8

Shaggy spun around and came face-to-face with the Skate Monster.

"ZOINKS!" Shaggy cried. "Run, Scoob!"

Scooby and Shaggy took off like nobody's business. The Skate Monster followed them around the top of the skate pit and then skated off into the shadows. As Shaggy and Scooby sat there panting, Fred, Daphne, and Velma ran over.

"Are you two all right?" Daphne asked.

Shaggy nodded.

"Good job finding that secret door," Fred said.

"Are you kidding?" Shaggy asked. "If we hadn't found that secret door, we never would've gotten chased by that rolling terror!"

"If you hadn't found that secret door, we never would have found this clue," Velma said. She held up a small rectangular object with tiny silver pins sticking out along the sides. The pins were all bent in the same direction and pointed to the ground.

"You found some staples?" Shaggy asked.

"They're not staples." Velma laughed. "This is a computer chip. And these tiny silver prongs attach the chip to the motherboard in a computer. Then the computer can run the program embedded within the chip."

"The only kinds of chips Scoob and I

are into are potato chips," Shaggy said. "Speaking of which, you didn't happen to come across any extra bags of chips up there on the judges' platform, did you?"

"Funny you should mention that," Fred said with a smile. "Why don't you and Scooby go see for yourself?"

"Now, why would we want to go all the way up there?" Shaggy asked.

"To help us capture the monster," Daphne explained. "What do you say?"

Shaggy and Scooby shook their heads in unison.

"We've seen that weirdo up close and personal two times too many," Shaggy said.

He and Scooby folded their arms in defiant resolve.

"Would you make it three times for a Scooby Snack?" Daphne asked.

Scooby's eyes lit up and his tail began wagging.

"Rou ret!" he barked.

Daphne tossed one of the treats in the air and Scooby gulped it down.

"Aaaaahhhhh," he said as a feeling of contentment filled his tummy.

Fred explained the plan. Shaggy and Scooby would pretend to judge another skateboard competition. To make it look real, Fred himself would skate into the pit. Daphne and Velma would hide with the big welcome banner just behind the railing. When the Skate Monster showed up in the pit, Fred would skate out of the way while Shaggy and Scooby drew the

monster's attention. Just as the monster made its way toward the judging platform, Daphne, Velma, and Fred would snare the creature in the welcome banner.

Everyone took their positions . . . even Shaggy and Scooby, who were not terribly happy about returning to the platform. But Scooby found one more unopened bag of potato chips that he and Shaggy shared to pass the time.

"This isn't so bad after all," Shaggy said.

Fred, meanwhile, skated around the half-pipe, trying his best to look like a professional skater. Sure enough, the Skate Monster showed up. It entered like before, by jumping over the rail and down into the half-pipe. After a few impressive twists, it began skating after Fred.

"Get ready!" Fred called as he maneuvered himself toward the stairs. "Now, Shaggy!"

Shaggy realized that was his cue to pick up the scorecards and show them to the monster. But his fingers were so greasy from the potato chips that he fumbled the cards. Scooby reached over to grab them before they fell down into the skate pit. But Scooby's paws were also greasy, and as he lost his balance he couldn't stop himself from falling.

Scooby tumbled over the railing and landed right on the Skate Monster's back. The monster wobbled under Scooby's weight but somehow managed to regain its balance. It soared up the half-pipe and jumped the rail, landing squarely

on the path. The monster picked up speed
and headed right for the archway over the
entrance.

"Duck, Scooby!" Daphne and Velma
shouted.

Scooby-Doo saw the archway coming
straight at him and ducked just in time. The
Skate Monster soared into Pollywog Park, spook-
ing people along the path.

"Relp! Raggy!" Scooby called.

By this time, Scooby had wrapped all of his paws around the Skate Monster's head, so there was no way for it to see where it was going. The monster somehow managed to remain on the path — the same path that Shaggy and Scooby had taken from the dock.

The Skate Monster rolled along the wooden dock and sailed off the end into Great Pollywog Pond. Scooby jumped off just in time and landed in a rowboat with two other people: the men in the green and brown suits.

Chapter 9

Fred got the creature out of the water with help from some of the dockhands. The men in the rowboat rowed Scooby back to shore. Everyone gathered around the soggy Skate Monster. Just as one of the dockhands was about to remove its mask, Daphne shouted, "Wait!"

She and Velma ran over with Sabrina Sargent.

"We found Sabrina tied up at the back of the snack bar," Daphne said. "Just behind the ice-cream freezer."

"See! I told you Scooby and I should've gone for ice cream before!" Shaggy joked.

"Sabrina, would you like to do the honors?" Velma asked.

"Absolutely," she said. She reached over and yanked off the Skate Monster's mask.

"Gregory Bly!" Sabrina gasped. "You? I was sure it was Wheels Trackman."

"So were we . . . at first," Daphne said.

"After all, who else could have executed all of those amazing skate moves?"

But as the gang explained the clues they'd found, Sabrina began to understand how it couldn't have been Wheels.

"You see, the first clue we found was an Arcadeland token," Fred said. "And we remembered that only a few people in the entire skate park would have one of those."

"Gregory Bly, for one," Sabrina said.

"That's right," Velma agreed. "But do you remember that Gregory told us he had given one to Wheels Trackman?"

Sabrina thought for a moment and nodded.

"And then later on, we met some odd woman who lives just behind the wall over there," Fred said.

Sabrina immediately knew whom he meant.

"You mean Mrs. Higgenbotham," Sabrina said.

"That's her," Shaggy said. "I never forget a name, especially one as strange as Higgiet Harriebotham."

"Anyway, she also had a token because she told us that Arcadeland was the only place she could go for some peace and quiet," Fred explained.

"But having three suspects doesn't seem very useful," Sabrina said.

"It's not," Daphne agreed. "That's why we kept looking for clues." She then showed Sabrina the monster's rhyme written on the back of the town's zoning bylaws.

"Why would someone have these bylaws?" Sabrina wondered aloud.

Velma explained that both Gregory Bly and

Harriet Higgenbotham were so upset with the skate park that they were looking for things the skate park did wrong so the town would have to shut it down.

"And that eliminated Wheels Trackman," Sabrina said, finally understanding that part of the mystery. "But how did you know it was Gregory Bly?"

"This last clue," Fred said. He showed Sabrina the computer chip and she immediately knew what it was for.

"This must be one of those Wheels Trackman video game chips that Gregory Bly told us about," she said.

Gregory Bly shivered beneath his soaking monster costume.

"You k-k-k-kids and your m-m-m-meddling m-m-mutt ruined my pl-pl-plans!" he shouted. "I was g-g-going to get rich with my new arc-c-c-cade g-g-g-games. But who will want to p-p-play my g-g-game when they can do the real thing in P-P-Pollywog Skaters' P-P-Paradise?

C-c-curse you all!" The police took Gregory Bly away and the crowd soon dispersed.

The men in the green and brown suits walked up to Sabrina.

"Sabrina Sargent?" the tall man in the green suit asked. She immediately knew who he was.

"Mr. Shooby! Mr. Scaggy!" she said. "I am so sorry for this terrible mix-up! Please accept my apologies."

"Forget about it," said Mr. Shooby, the man in the brown suit with the blue and yellow handkerchief in the pocket. "If we had been there, we would've been right in the middle of this mess."

"And we never would have been able to do what these kids have done," Mr. Scaggy added.

Sabrina turned to the gang with a big smile on her face.

"You rescued me and saved the skate park!" she said. "I can't thank you — especially you, Scooby — enough!"

"Sure you can," Shaggy replied, stepping forward. "All we ever wanted is a little ice cream, right, pal?"

"Scooby-Dooby-Doo!" cheered Scooby as he skated down the dock on Sabrina's skateboard.